Arlo Bates

Berries of the Brier

Arlo Bates

Berries of the Brier

ISBN/EAN: 9783337419196

Printed in Europe, USA, Canada, Australia, Japan

Cover: Foto ©Andreas Hilbeck / pixelio.de

More available books at **www.hansebooks.com**

BERRIES OF THE BRIER.

BERRIES OF THE BRIER.

ARLO BATES.

BOSTON:

ROBERTS BROTHERS.

1886.

University Press:

John Wilson and Son, Cambridge.

To the Memory

of

"Eleanor Putnam."

CONTENTS.

———•———

CONTENTS.

BERRIES OF THE BRIER.

MEMORIES OF CUBA.

I.

UNA SEÑORITA.

ONE found a reason, when she came,
　　Why the *Pasco* glowed with light,
And why the music swelled and thrilled
　　As if upon a festal night.

The band was playing *Le Désir*, —
　　Why that old strain I cannot tell, —
And all her carriage, all her grace,
　　Accorded with the music well.

High overhead the southern moon
　　Shone as no other moon can shine ;
Perhaps I fixed her liquid glance,
　　Perhaps 't was but a fancy mine ;

And yet in northern climes and far,
　The scene before me rises clear;
Her gracious shape I seem to see
　Whene'er the band plays *Le Désir!*

II.

A SONG OF REVERY.

BENEATH the heavy northern skies,
　That hang so low, some subtle sense
Is well aware how placid lies
　A blue lagoon, in calm intense,
　　Glassing the heaven high and far.
　　Ah, love, how keen thy memories are!

How soft the bamboo shadows fall,
　And palm-trees wave with rhythmic beat,
While lizards up the sunny wall
　Dart in swift joyance of the heat,
　　As burning shines the mid-world sun.
　　Ah, love, how soon thy joys are done!

How well my dream her lattice knows,
　Which from the blinding tropic day

Shuts in sweet dusk and scents of rose
   And more delights than words might say,
   Which I shall never know again.
   How bitter love's regrets and vain!

III.

ON THE ROAD TO CHORRERA.

[1790.]

THREE horsemen galloped the dusty way
   While sun and moon were both in the sky;
An old crone crouched in the cactus' shade,
   And craved an alms as they rode by.
     A friendless hag she seemed to be,
     But the queen of a bandit crew was she.

One horseman tossed her a scanty dole,
   A scoffing couplet the second trolled,
But the third, from his blue eyes frank and free,
   No glance vouchsafed the beldam old;
     As toward the sunset and the sea,
     No evil fearing, rode the three.

A curse she gave for the pittance small,
  A gibe for the couplet's ribald word ;
But that which once had been her heart
  At sight of the silent horseman stirred :
    And safe through the ambushed band they speed
    For the sake of the rider who would not heed !

IV.

THE *DANZA.*

IF you never have danced the *danza*,
  With its wondrous rhythmic swirl,
While close to your bosom panted
  Some dark-eyed Creole girl,
    Of dancing you know naught !
    By Inez I was taught.

'T is a dance with strangest pauses,
  It moves as the breezes blow :
Her lips were like pomegranate blossoms,
  While her teeth were white as snow.
    Of beauty I knew naught ;
    By Inez I was taught.

The fountain splashed in the garden
  Where the palm-trees hid the moon ;
Who well had danced the *danza*,
  A kiss might crave as boon.
     Of loving I knew naught ;
     By Inez I was taught !

A WOMAN'S REJECTION.

THERE was one moment, sir,
   My soul unveiled her face,
And met your eyes with hers,
   Unflinching in her place.

Why did your glance avoid?
   Why did your eyelids fall?
There was the chance to prove
   Your manhood once for all!

But since you failed of that,
   Go; be blest or forlorn;
To me you count no more
   Than you had ne'er been born.

BETWEEN.

HOW fare the hosts of the dead,
　　Or of those that are still to be,
While holding the hands of these unseen,
　　Shivering between, stand we?

Wailing from deeps of the dark
　　We come, and wailing go
To deeps of the outer dark again,
　　In endless column slow.

The listless hands of the dead
　　We clasp with frantic strain, —
Do the unborn kiss with tears our hands,
　　Seeking response in vain?

INITIATION.

OUT of the Unknown came I,
 Pure-hearted, free from guile ;
A mystic maiden met me
 And bewitched me with her smile.

She taught me deadly secrets
 It breaks the heart to know :
Ah, Life ! how had I wronged thee
 That thou should'st harm me so?

THE BROWN LICHEN.

WITH dusky fingers clinging to the stone,
　　Through summer's languid days and lovely
　　　　nights,
Through autumn's chillness and the spring's delights,
　　The lichen lives in grimmest state, alone.

The spicy summer breezes o'er it go,
But from its nun-like breast win no perfume ;
Brown bees, gold-dusted, seek some flower's bloom,
　　Nor pause above it, flitting to and fro.

The snail glides over it with solemn pace ;
The cunning spider in it spins her snare ;
But, be its tenants either foul or fair,
　　The lichen naught is troubled in her place.

The fays full oft in splendid state go by,
And elfin laughter thrills through all the air,
" What cheer, Dame Lichen, grave and debonair ? "
To them vouchsafes the lichen no reply.

We pluck among the crannies of the stone
The wild flowers, purple, golden, or sweet blue ;
But both in nature and in friendship too,
We leave the grim brown lichen quite alone.

A WOODLAND TRAGEDY.

A ROSE leaned over a woodland pool,
  With its own imaged beauty thrilling;
So self-entranced, it had no eye
For daffodilly or lily cool,
Or bending grasses or dragon-fly
On wings of opal flitting by,
Or clouds the heaven filling.

There strayed a maiden the woodland through,
Her image in that mirror flinging.
The rose's blissful dreams swift fled;
Its beauty far outshone it knew;
Shivered in all its petals red
And on the pool their richness shed. —
The maiden passed on singing.

CUPID'S LINEAGE.

WITH Cupid as once I chatted,
    ' Fair Aphrodite's son '
By chance I called the naughty rogue ;
    When retorted the volatile one :

" 'T is time to unlearn those fancies,
    Those myths are false and vain :
Sir Idlesse was my father named,
    And my mother was Lady Disdain."

A SHADOW BOAT.

UNDER my keel another boat
　　Sails as I sail, floats as I float ;
Silent and dim and mystic still,
It steals through that weird nether-world,
Mocking my power, though at my will
The foam before its prow is curled,
Or calm it lies, with canvas furled.

Vainly I peer, and fain would see
What phantom in that boat may be ;
Yet half I dread, lest I with ruth
Some ghost of my dead past divine,
Some gracious shape of my lost youth,
Whose deathless eyes once fixed on mine
Would draw me downward through the brine !

A FANTASY.

IF there were a thousand years
    Between my life and me,
And as in an age-dim tome
    I might its story see, —

How mystic and sweet and strange,
    Like some old tale, would be
The anguish that now I know,
    In my hopeless love for thee !

METEMPSYCHOSIS.

'MID the sea-silt and the sea-sand,
    Sinuous and sinister, fold on fold,
Sliding and winding tortuously,
Slips the sea-snake, weird and old ;
    Longing, with gleams of slumbrous fire
    In her dull eyes, and fierce desire
    In her slow brain, for that far time
When, rising lotus-like from ooze and slime,
Her sinuate litheness changed to supple grace,
Her sibilance melted to witching speech,
She shall the heights of glorious being reach,
And lure her prey with woman's form and face.

A LOVER'S MESSENGERS.

THE earliest flowers of spring
   To thee, beloved, I bring:

Anemone and graceful adder's-tongue,
With golden cowslips, yellow as the sun
And fresh as brooks by which they sprung;
Sweet violets that we love; and, one by one,
The blossoms that come after, — cherry-bloom
And snow of shad-bush, wilful columbine
In pale red raiment, and the milky stars
Of chickweed-wintergreen; the trilliums fine
That make the robins sing; slim walnut-buds
In satin sheen, and furry curling ferns,
Like owlets half awake; with floods
Of alder tassels that drop dust of gold
On the dark pools where, 'twixt the bars
Of piercing sunbeams, speckled troutlings dart.

And thus until the jocund year is old
And frosts spin cerements, white and chill,
O'er all the woodlands, fold on fold,
I tell the days with flowers, to mind thee still
Who, kind to blossoms, to me cruel art,
How swift is time, how constant is my heart.

FAILURE.

COUNT not the trampled dead spared any strain
   Because another won where he was slain.
Are hearts ignoble proved whose cause is lost?
Vain is the standard if success hide cost.

Loss is not failure ; not success is gain ;
Idle as measures are both bliss and pain.
Who falters, fails, although he clutch the prize ;
Who proves his utmost, wins, though dead he lies.

A SKETCH-BOOK BY THE SEA.

ON THE BEACH.

A LEVEL sea to the edge of the world,
　　Purple and green and gray as steel ;
A fisher-boat with its white sails furled,
　　And a far black ledge where flock the seal.

A WINDY DAY.

As silver 'neath the smith's quick beat
　　Gleam the reflections on the bay,
Pale, trampled fires that have no heat,
　　By the wind crushed from gold to gray.

THE STARBOARD TACK.

The breeze is stiff as the schooner tacks,
　　And quick each dusky, hollow sail
Crinkles like satin in the sun,
　　Gleaming like beaten silver mail.

ON THE LEDGE.

In ineffable floods of beryl
   The wave pours over the ledge ;
Chrysoprase, pearl, and nacre
   It heaps on the rock's black edge.

AN OLD GARDEN.

A dim old garden, where is primly set
   Row after row of box and lupine pale,
With quaint old flowers that modern times forget ;
   Where honeysuckles from the trellis trail,

And stiff and tall along the shoreward rocks
   Lombardy poplars woful sentry stand,
And each with shadow on the greensward mocks
   The spectral pointing of the dial's hand, —

The dial that on carvèd post of red
   Marks all the wasting of each sunny hour,
But when the sea and sky are gray as lead,
   Has neither hope nor comfort in its power.

A NIGHT SKETCH.

Upon the sea the pictured moon
   Floats like a golden shell ;
On the dark sky their mystic rune
   The constellations spell.

Afar a single silver sail
   Has through the mist-wreaths broke,
Like some lost spirit, wan and pale,
That strives toward heaven without avail,
   To climb on incense smoke.

CAMPOBELLO,
   September, 1885.

A LOVER'S CANTICLES.

I.

AUBADO.

IN the hush of the morn, before the sun,
   I waken to think of thee ;
And all the sweet day thus begun
   As hallowed seems to be.

In the holy repose the morning star
   With trembling awaits the sun,
And thus my heart, if near or far,
   Awaits thee, sweetest one.

In a golden ecstasy of bliss
   The fair morning-star will die ;
But I, immortal by thy kiss,
   Live but when thou art nigh.

II.

SONG.

WERE I a prince Egyptian, countless years
    Swathed in fine linen, cased in cedarn pride,
With spicery and balsams all enwrapt,
    Adorned with gold and with vermilion dyed, —

Yet should thy lightest footfall stir the air
    Of that dim chamber where I lay at rest,
Through all my being would love tremors thrill,
    And hot my longing heart leap in my breast.

III.

MEMNON.

SPEECHLESS through all the cheerless night
    Stood Memnon's statue ; but at morn
The stone lips hailed the Day-god bright
    With sounds of love and rapture born.

Lo ! here an image of my heart,
 That has no voice bereft of thee ;
But into songs of joy must start
 If thy sweet presence shine on me.

IV.

THE ROSE GUERDON.

I KISS the rosebud which you wore,
 Yet know not why I love it so ;
'T was but a simple flower before
It blushed against thy breast of snow.

But since, to such a worth 't is grown,
It is a guerdon most divine ;
Because the touch which it has known,
The breast which it has pressed, were thine.

V.

THE RING.

THIS ring I send thee thrice a thousand years
    Lay buried 'mid the dust of Lybian kings.
If it might speak, unto our eager ears,
What strange tales would it tell of bygone things, —

" Wild, shifting scenes " of mystery and pride,
The pomp of monarchs long forgotten now ;
But all its tales must seem as naught beside
The one it brings thee, — Love's eternal vow !

VI.

SERENADE.

WHILE stars above thee glow,
    And the red moon sinks low
Into the dusky sea ;
Night visions come and go :
Dearest, in dreaming so
Dream'st thou who loveth thee?

Weirdly the night-bird sings,
Sailing on silent wings
Over the dewy lea ;
Her note a rapture brings :
Sweetest, with heavenly things
Dream'st thou who loveth thee ?

Deep longing fills his breast ;
Knows he nor sleep nor rest,
Severed as now from thee :
Fairest one, loved the best,
Were the sweet truth confessed,
Dream'st thou who loveth thee ?

VII.

DEVOTION.

I.

NO lotus on Ganges floating
   With thy beauty may compare ;
The moon over Eden gloating
Saw nothing half so fair.

More bright than stars that glimmer,
 Lingering o'er some snowy peak
Morn-crimsoned, thine eyes shimmer
 Above thy faint flushed cheek.

As blindness yearns for seeing,
 As Ganges longs for the sea,
As the poet's dream for being,
 So longs my heart for thee !

II.

No lotus on Ganges floating,
 Trembling in dewy sleep,
Above the sacred waters
 That ever seaward sweep,

Is purer than thy pureness,
 Is whiter than thy thought,
Is sweeter than thy presence,
 Or more with blessing fraught.

As worships the Hindoo the river
 Where the snowy lilies be,
So with all pure devotion
 My spirit worships thee !

VIII.

SELF-REPROACH.

WHEN first death's great delight I met,
　　There might, beloved, one instant be
I should forget — no, not forget,
　　But not have conscious thought of thee.

And all eternity, contrite,
　　I should be striving to atone
For that oblivion, till aright
　　My heart remembered thee alone!

IX.

CONSTANCY.

THE weakest heart, whate'er its changes,
　　Howe'er the varying life may run,
Howe'er the light affection ranges,
　　Is constant in its depths to one.

Through sweetest lands the stranger wanders,
  Yet none of all like home he sees ;
On many a maid his fancy squanders,
  But gives his heart to none of these.

By night and day a constant yearning
  Burns in his soul for one afar ;
To her his thoughts still backward turning,
  As the fond needle seeks its star.

The lightest heart, whate'er its changes,
  Until this fitful life be done,
Howe'er the fickle fancy ranges,
  Is constant in its love to one.

A REVERSING MIRROR.

MY love, if we sat at the play,
    And our story were acted true,
Would the hero win only the scorn
    Which now you mete out as my due?

I fancy you then would relent,
    Or even your censure rue ;
And, indeed, I cannot be sure
    But I, too, might exonerate you !

LISA'S GATE.

TWO lovers meet at Lisa's gate :
    " Comrade, comrade, who art thou?
The night is dark, the hour is late,
No welcomes here thy coming wait ;
    Comrade, comrade, speed thee now ! "

Two broadswords clash in sudden fight :
    " Comrade, comrade, who art thou?
Thy sword-thrusts fall with bitter might,
Nor thou nor I shall see the light.
    Comrade, comrade, speed thee now ! "

Fair Lisa hears their dying cry :
    " Comrade, comrade, who art thou? "
As idle breath it passes by ;
To one afar she wafts a sigh :
    " Comrade, comrade, speed thee now ! "

UNCHOSEN.

STILL stings one bitter moment
    When — in that mystic land
Where, waiting Fate's dread summons,
    The unborn spirits stand —

Genius walked grand among us,
    Her own to signify ;
And while I thrilled with yearning,
    Smiled on me, but passed by !

A LAST WORD.

IF I forgive you, forego you, forget you,
   Is that the whole?   Do you therefore go free?
My sorrow is all my life to regret you:
Have you no pang in remembering me?

'T is not for love the memory should pain you,
You will not think if my wounded heart bleed;
But for yourself, that dishonor should stain you, —
Surely that thought might be worthy your heed.

Though I forgive you, I may not absolve you,
Only repentance your guilt can remove.
I plead by dead love; in self-pity revolve you
How yet remorse your atonement may prove!

A LAMENT.

LET gleeful muses sing their roundelays !
    So might my muse have sung ;
      But in the jocund days
        When she was young,
      She chanced upon a grave
New-made, and since, there strays
A mournful cadence through her lightest stave.

      Her mask, however gay,
      Still covers cheeks tear-wet ;
      She cannot, in her singing, smile
      Until she can forget.

TO THE PHŒBE BIRD.

E ACH blessed morning,
  Much to my scorning,
You 're up and wailing for Phœbe dear ;
  And still your calling,
  When day is falling,
Doleful as ever salutes the ear.

  We all admire
  The constant fire
Supposed to burn in lover's breast ;
  Yet glints of reason
  May do no treason
To faith and love and all the rest.

  This endless sighing,
  These threats of dying,
Only provoke the maiden's scorn ;

'T is arrant folly
Not to be jolly
Despite of any maid that 's born !

Your mournful wailing
Is unavailing ;
You 'd more effect if you should swear !
This heartless Phœbe —
Whoever *she* be —
For all your sighs will nothing care.

Why don't you flout her,
And vow you doubt her,
And rate her for an arrant jade ?
You 'd soon subdue her
If so you 'd woo her :
She 'll never love till she 's afraid.

You, silly songster,
Protest, " Thou wrong'st her ! "
But I 've been longer born than you ;
I know the sex, sir,
Their tricks to vex, sir :
Flame when you scorn, ice when you sue !

ONE.

THE world is naught till one is come
    Who is the world ; then beauty wakes
And voices sing that have been dumb.

The world is naught when one is gone
    Who was the world ; then the heart breaks
That this is lost which once was won.

Dear love, this life, so passion fraught,
    From you its bliss or sorrow takes ;
With you is all ; without you naught.

MIGHT LOVE BE BOUGHT.

MIGHT love be bought, I were full fain
    My all to give thy love to gain.
      Yet would such getting profit naught ;
      Possession with keen fears were fraught
Would make even love's blisses vain.

For who could tell what god might deign
His golden treasures round thee rain,
      Till ruin to my hopes were brought,
        Might love be bought.

Better a pensioner remain
On thy dear grace, since to attain
      To worthiness in vain I sought.
      Thy kindness hath assurance wrought
Could never be between us twain,
        Might love be bought.

´SOLITUDE.

Dangerous is solitude : so easily
   We mingle dreams with deeds, and what we would
   Set down as what we do ; our hardihood
Untried, call courage ; and to seem, to be.

Self must with men its value measured see,
   Its deeds with deeds the ages mark as good.
   Must flee self-pity ; oft "misunderstood"
Means mere misunderstanding.   Equity

Though hard yet sure, life brings.   Whate'er excuse
   Self plead with self, to fail is still to fail ;
And so the world scores, though the fond recluse

Dream high intents no less than acts prevail.
   Life 's energy or naught ; let it have use,
Consume in deeds, not in mere prayers exhale !

4

A SPRING FANCY.

THE first spring bird sang blithely
    In a meadow scarcely green,
Where the soft leaves covered fondly
    A violet not yet seen.

The bird flew high in ether,
    But the song was not lost in air ;
'T was out-breathed in sweetest odors
    By the violet springing there.

A FEAR.

MUTE, walking grief-stricken with wringing hands,
　　Among the living, countless spirits go,
And jostle in the crowds the friends they seek,
　　While neither may the other's presence know.

Lovers, death-severed, wander side by side
　　Unknowing, rent with keenest throes of pain ;
And side by side walk friends who, each for each,
　　Waste life lamenting with sighs long as vain.

For spirit sense can naught but spirits ken,
　　While we, clay-bound, see only fellow clay ;
Yet time our grief assuages, we forget,
　　While faithful to a deathless memory they !

A CASUISTRY.

WE promised each to each that day
    Not what we said, but what we were;
If time has seen our love decay,
    We both are blameless, I aver.

Its rich bloom gives the rose of June
    Until it fades: it can no more;
Its linkèd sweetness breathes the tune
    And dies as waves waste on the shore.

Is rose or song or love untrue
    That it immortal cannot be?
Some law of being running through
    They all obey; no less must we.

We were unwise, that may be said;
    But now absolved, each goes his way:
As easy wake the rose that's dead
    As now keep vows were made that day!

CONTENT.

CONTENTED lie the noontime resting herd ;
Content are dotards, nodding heads of snow ;
Content are prattling babes, too young to know
The hopes by which the mother's heart is stirred.

But strong men, fired with zeal unswerving, gird
Their loins with patience and to battle go ;
Their souls with yearning filled, little they know
Of lotus-fed content ! The soaring bird

Sees still new deeps above, and longing sends
Her song aspiring toward those loftier skies
She may not reach ; and heroes, unto ends

Beyond attaining, strive with eager eyes,
In godlike effort that as far transcends
Poor dull content as heaven an earthly prize !

PRESENT JOY.

COULD I taste the joy of to-morrow,
    Of to-morrow and yesterday, —
The bliss shall assuage coming sorrow,
    And the bliss that has passed away, —
From these at last might I borrow
    True sense of joy to-day.

A LOVE-SONG.

L OVE 'S like the eglantine, which bears
     The sweetest rose,
Whose witching perfume flows
     On summer airs.

Ardent youth longs with eager hand
     To pluck the flower,
And many a wistful hour
     Will sighing stand.

Yet if his fortune bring him nigh
     To grasp the rose,
Only its thorn he knows, —
     The bloom gone by !

THE LOST DREAM.

I WOKE in the pulseless night,
　And a sweet dream stole away
So near that its wings in flight
　Shed perfume where I lay.

And ne'er in this life of mine
　Can that loss amended be,
Since now I can only divine
　How sweet was that dream of thee.

HILAD TO MARGERY.

I.

I SAW to-day a merry, smooth-faced maid
　　Laughing, and basking brown cheeks in the sun ;
And memory at the token, one by one,
Repeated all your words, and thereby laid

New meaning on them. " Why," you said, " invade
　　My girlhood's garden? Till the spring is done
　　I list the birds, and will be wooed of none.
You fright my finches, and you cast a shade

Upon my violets. Than your love their bloom
　　Is fairer. Leave me, then." And I in shame
And grief made way, and gave the finches room.

And when to-day I saw this maid, there came
　　A wonder o'er me how I dared presume
Break up your peace to press my passion's claim.

II.

I wronged thee that I let my shadow fall
   Across thy sunshine, that I weakly let
   Around thee steal the chill of my regret ;
Not unto thee should I have raised the pall

Which covered my dead hopes.   And still in all
   'T was love, that, missing love's fruition, yet
   Must claim the seal of recognition set
As being love, pure love, nor mean nor small.

It asked but if thou feltest its shy touch
   Upon thy garment's hem, thou count it not
Pollution, and it surely asked not much,

Since mankind's weakest, howso low his lot,
   May love his God, who counts that love as such
It gives His glory lustre, not a spot.

III.

No boon, no restitution did I claim
   For all the love I lavished upon thee ;
   Since as the sun must shine, e'en so with me
" To live " includes " to love," being the same.

By inner sweetness, spite of outward blame,
  Love works its own completeness if it be
  In king or churl. Oft coarse and ill to see
Has been the vase from which with odors came

  The richest balsam ; rough the new-hewn tomb,
In that Judæan garden, where they laid
  The body of the Lord in doubt and gloom ;

Yet as that corse, with nails and spear-thrust frayed,
  Made holy all the place that gave it room,
So hallows love the heart its home is made.

A WINTER TWILIGHT.

Pale beryl sky, with clouds
    Hued like dove's wing,
    O'ershadowing
    The dying day,
And whose edge half enshrouds
    The first fair evening star,
    Most crystalline by far
Of all the stars that night enring,
    Half human in its ray :
What blessed, soothing sense of calm
Comes with this twilight, — sovereign balm
    That takes at last the bitter sting
    Of day's keen pain away.

HEREDITY.

THOUGH half his suit she favored,
   Yet did she turn away.
What weakness in him lay
  To fail her will to stay?
Alas ! his grandsire wavered
  When his sweetheart said him nay.

TEKEL.

IF he had stabbed me where I stood,
  So dear he was, I could have died
Without a doubt that, somehow, good
    He must have meant, though space denied
    To show what ill would else betide.

But when at my worst need his glance,
    That should have held me up, star-clear,
Turned but the faintest thought askance,
    No more he was my friend, nor dear
    Could be, were loneness ne'er so drear.

IN THY CLEAR EYES.

IN thy clear eyes, fairest, I see
　Sometimes of love a transient glow ;
But ere my heart assured may be,
With cold disdain thou mockest me :
　Hope fades as songs to silence flow.

Ah ! most bewitching, mocking she,
　Fairer than poet's dream may show,
The glance of scorn how can I dree
　　In thy clear eyes?

　Life is so brief, and to and fro
Like thistledown above the lea
　Fly our poor days ; then why so slow
　To bend from pride?　Let us bliss know
Ere age the light dims ruthlessly
　　In thy clear eyes.

A NIGHT RIDE.

HIS swart cheek tingled with the rain,
　So swift he rode that night ;
But all his speed no boon might gain
Save to kiss, in a rapture of love and pain,
　Dead lips at morning light.

Had he but known, what touched his cheek,
　Riding that midnight wild,
Was her soul's kiss that might not speak,
And the wail in his ear, so woeful and weak,
　The cry of his unborn child !

THE SECOND-SIGHT.

" I have the second-sight, Goethe." — BETTINA.

TWICE in his life has man the second-sight.
　　First does young love give prescience divine,
As when the tender springtide moon benign
Pours o'er the wanderer floods of golden light,

Revealing gracious forms that troop by night
　　From haunt of elf and fay.　Next, when decline
The stars of love, and in the western brine
Plunge darkling, then, with wonder and affright,

The heart strays, like a seer with purpose dread
　　Who walks in storm-rent night along the plain
Of some old battle, and while round his head

Wild shrieks the wind, calls up the awful train
　　That know alike the fate of quick and dead ;
For woe, love's vision lost, gives second-sight again.

5

A ROSE.

[TRIOLETS.]

'TWAS a Jacqueminot rose
 That she gave me at parting;
Sweetest flower that blows
'Twas, a Jacqueminot rose.
In the lone garden close,
 With the swift blushes starting,
'Twas a Jacqueminot rose
 That she gave me at parting.

If she kissed it, who knows —
 Since I will not discover,
And lone is that close —
If she kissed it, who knows?
Or if not the red rose,
 Perhaps then the lover!
If she kissed it, who knows,
 Since I will not discover?

Yet at least with the rose
  Went a kiss that I 'm wearing !
More I will not disclose ;
Yet at least with the rose
Went *whose* kiss no one knows,
  Since I 'm only declaring
That at least with the rose
  Went a kiss that I 'm wearing !

HIS FATE.

WITH keenest mother-pain and mother-joy,
  With all that love could give or gold could buy,
Came into happy life a blue-eyed boy
  Under the azure of a Northern sky.

And who might know that in a wayside shed,
  Beneath the splendors of a Southern sun,
That self-same hour, upon a beggar's bed,
  His fate and ruin, her life too begun.

A CORYPHÉE.

IT was chalk and rouge, I knew,
  And the costumer's petty art;
And yet as the ballet you floated through
  I felt a thrill at my heart, —

A caprice of vague delight
  And a promise all sweet and vain;
Unless the frail bond of your dance to-night
  Shall bring us together again.

You have touched a chord in my breast, —
  Or a something that might be you, —
And I wonder if thus shall unbalanced rest
  The reckoning between us two;

Or if somewhere, face to face,
   Or dead or alive as may chance,
At last I shall pay all the debt of grace
   I owe for the joy of that dance.

Let it be whene'er it will,
   And the place be whate'er it may,
Be sure that my service to utmost shall be
   All yours in the deeds of that day.

LIFE.

LIFE is a ray of light
  Piercing dim air,
Whose motes, an instant bright,
  Tell that the beam is there.

A moment, and the golden gleam is gone ;
Yet who knows why, or whither fleeting on?

TRUTH.

A MAN knelt through the livelong night
   And prayed with tears that morn might rise :
The first beam of the waited light
   With cureless blindness smote his eyes.

A soul in darkness cried for truth,
   And dreamed the truth its bliss should be.
Ah ! sad mistake, provoking ruth !
   The truth brought endless misery.

TO A GHOST.

OF old, if thy robe but brushed me,
　　How did I start and thrill !
The simple, dimmest memory
　　Has power to pain me still !
Yet now as I stand and see thee,
　　Those fervors all have fled ;
I burned in thy living presence,
　　But thou canst not move me, dead.

And yet those eyes still sparkle,
　　Still glows that hair of gold,
Still breathes the Indian perfume
　　From thy robe's silken fold ;
Thy voice has the old-time music,
　　So sweet that it moved my dread, —
No, thou art still of the living ;
　　It is I who am of the dead !

AN INDIAN AIR.

CARELESS upon a time-stained lute
   I played a subtile Indian air
That all the world forgets, but I,
   For love of one so sweetly fair,
     Who sang it once, remember.

The tune to plaintive moods did suit,
   Cadence to cadence melting slow;
Longings that not for time would die
   The music waked to softest glow,
     As brightens some dim ember.

The ghostly moon from midnight sky
   Peered shivering my dim lattice through;
A hound howled, and his cry told well
   Some spirit sought that spot anew
     Where its heart-love yet lingered.

A soft wind seemed to pass me by,
   Strange bliss a moment soothed my pain.
Why my tears sprang I might not tell ;
   But when I wiped those salt drops vain,
     The lute played on unfingered !

FROM THE GRAVE.

IN the castle garden a rose
   Had a hidden grave in its keeping :
With pallid babe on her breast,
   A mother bent over it weeping.

Never kiss of a father's lip
   Had brought to the babe its blessing
Till the mother that red rose laid
   Against its cheek, caressing.

RECOGNITION.

LOVER and mistress, sleeping side by side,
　　Death smote at once ; and in the outer air,
Amazedly confronted, each to each,
　　Their spirits stood, of all disguises bare.

With sudden loathing stung, one spirit fled,
　　Crying : " Love turns to hate if this be thou ! "
" Ah, stay ! " the other wailed, in swift pursuit ;
　　" Thee I have never truly loved till now ! "

"FELICISSIMA NOTTE."

UNDER the soft Italian moon
    We wished each other " happiest night,"
And went our ways ; and both alike
Were helpless in Fate's hand of might.

" The happiest night ; " for well we knew
Italian nights have more than dreams,
And too had learned that, truly seen,
All is not bliss that fairest seems !

For him the swift stiletto stab :
The warmth of clinging arms for me ;
Yet who might say whether had won
The happiest night, or I or he?

CONSOLATION.

IN days of anguish and of desolation
　　Say not : " Time shall assuage the smart ! "
Give to our grief at least the consecration
　　Of standing unmatched and apart.

" Ye shall forget."　Oh, bitter consolation,
　　More cruel than the woe it comes to heal,
That makes a mockery of lamentation,
　　And but the actor's cue each pang we feel !

Rent with the awful wrench of separation,
　　Leave us at least the dignity of pain ;
Though it be false beyond all reparation,
　　Let us believe we cannot love again !

1883.

H. R. P.

"Gone into the world of light."
HENRY VAUGHAN.

ART thou called higher to a world of light
    Alone, while we in outer dark remain?
We catch vague gleams of glory through our pain,
As of the stars half seen in some drear night,

And with a love would supplement our sight,
    Strive to see clearer. Do we hear a strain
    Of sweetest sound, like welcoming refrain?
Ah! if it be that when in sore affright

We thought the place that held thee was a tomb,
    It was that bright world's portal, we can wait
Until we too from out this doubtful gloom

Are bidden thither. Ever first calls fate
    The worthiest. Oh, favored guest, some room,
Some memory keep for us, though we be late!

THE BALLAD OF THE SPINNER.

I.

I.

THE Spinner sought the highest room,   *Of the*
   As downward sank the sun ;   *Spinner.*
She took her wheel amid the gloom,
   And swift and deft she spun.

"He is false !" she said upon the stair ;
   "Ah, false !" as grew the thread.
She startled the chill silence there
   With murmured words of dread.

She drew the flax out fine and long ;
   To a wild, wistful lay,
She twisted into troubled song
   A spell strange powers obey.

II.

Of the Sailor. NOTHING of ill the Sailor dreamed,
    Watching the sun go down ;
To see his sweet new love, he seemed,
    Sewing her wedding-gown.

How slow for him his boat did go,
    How dragged the hours along,
Till he again her voice should know,
    Singing some well-loved song.

Out on the sea, pauseless as doom,
    The sure tides flood and run ;
There in the tower's highest room
    The Spinner sang and spun.

II.

I.

WHEN at the sunset, on the land,
   The Spinner climbed the stair,
Over the sea on either hand,
   The sky of cloud was bare.

Of the Spell.

But as she drew the fatal thread,
   Low, moaning winds were blown ;
And as she chanted words of dread,
   Pale, fitful lightnings shone.

II.

THE Sailor's golden love-dreams fled ;
   Within his troubled mind
Remembered he, with sudden dread,
   The Spinner left behind.

How the Spell wrought upon the Sea.

With sudden darkness fell the night
  Like fate upon the sea ;
The winds rushed on with gathering might ;
  In deadly fear sailed he.

Swift, fervid flashes from the sky
  Burned out amid the dark ;
Strange, fiery sparkles from the sea
  His vessel's course did mark.

Blue, lurid lights along the shrouds
  Like charnel bale-fires glowed ;
Most direful moanings filled the air,
  The coming wreck to bode.

The opal stone in the Spinner's ring,
  Upon the Sailor's hand
Gleamed through the night with sinister light,
  And shone like an altar brand.

Then straight the Spinner far away
  He saw in vision clear ;
Above the storm her droning wheel
  Buzzed dizzy in his ear.

Out on the sea, pauseless as doom,
   The sure tides flood and run ;
While in the tower's highest room
   The Spinner sang and spun.

III.

I.

An instant, as the day declined,
   The Spinner left her wheel ;
An instant lulled the bitter wind
   And hushed the thunder's peal.

*The Spinner
setteth a
Lure-Light.*

She placed before the lattice dim
   A taper's lighted star,
That through the wild night shone to him
   Resistless from afar.

It called his bark along the sea
   In spite of helm and oar,
Until he heard upon the lee
   The breakers' hungry roar.

II.

Of the
nameless
Shapes the
Spell
aroused.

WHAT sights the lightning showed around,
  As on toward death he drave !
He shrieks as one who breaks his swound,
  Borne living to his grave.

For countless hungry, slimy shapes
  That writhe in the wild sea
Swarmed through the foam of surf-lashed capes,
  And he their prey should be !

Out on the sea, pauseless as doom,
  The sure tides flood and run ;
While in the tower's highest room
  The Spinner sang and spun.

IV.

I.

THE Spinner heard the Sailor's cry,
    Amid her fatal song ;
And knew thereby his bark drew nigh,
    Drawn by her spells along.

The Spinner
almost
relenteth.

She shuddereth, as who in death
    Sees some most loved one laid ;
But still she saith, with panting breath :
    "Ah, false one ! Ah, betrayed !"

II.

YET once again the Sailor cried,
    And called the Spinner's name :
On her white lips the wild song died ; —
    She quenched the taper's flame ;

She relenteth
quite, but too
late.

His voice once dear called from afar,
　　And love, though turned to hate,
Grasps still the soul it once did hold
　　With clasp as strong as fate.

She pressed her heart in bitter pain,
　　Her heart that would relent ;
She strove in vain to chant again
　　The spell of fell intent.

And with such moan as they may make
　　The pains of hell who feel,
The magic thread too late she brake,
　　And stopped the fatal wheel.

Out on the sea, pauseless as doom,
　　Did sure tides flood and run ;
While in the tower's highest room
　　The Spinner sang and spun.

V.

I.

THE sun rose red in the morning mists
   And tinged the flying scud,
And flecked the floating sea-gull's breast
   With spots that shone like blood.

*Of what
the rising
Sun shone
upon.*

Its light decked all the broken wreck
   With mellow radiance fair,
And turned to pearl each flake of foam
   On the drowned Sailor's hair.

II.

AND in that chamber like a dream,
   Snared in her broken thread,
Its dusky beam touched with its gleam
   The Spinner, lying dead.

*The Fate
of the
Spinner.*

Out on the sea, pauseless as doom,
   Still slow tides flood and run ;
But in the tower's highest room
   Nevermore maiden spun.

AQUA DELLA TOFFANA.

[ITALY; A.D. 16—.]

THE night is close and dark; the rain
    Beats on the rose.   Lit by my casement's glow,
Burns on the rose's beauty like a spark
Amid the gloom, although the nightingale
Shelters himself, and will not come to woo.

Is love then but a mood?   Merely a bliss
Of calms, that, like the stars, flees from the gloom
Of storms?   Or does the rose the long night through
Feel, though so far, the nightingale's hot breast
Throbbing with passion?

                    Ah, it must be so!
I feel my lover's heart, through night and rain,
Beating afar with pulses that make way
Into my very soul!

                    He sends me here
A tiny vial.

            "Love, I give you this,"
His words, "as giving you at once yourself
And me.   If in his lordship's wine — perchance
Such things have been — a drop should hap to fall,
He sleeps the sooner; and to you and me
What cause for grief if he forget to wake?"

What does it matter, O my rose?   Men die
As leaves fall, when we most would have them stay;
If sometimes from the bough where it will cling
We pluck a lingering leaf, long dry and sere,
What harm?   The bough is fairer, and the leaf
Was ready for the worm.   Is it for me,
Meek-eyed, to play the slave?   Though, like the queen
Aurelian led in chains, I feel my hands
In manacles, my soul is free as air!

Not one would ask upon my bridal morn
Whether my heart was his who came
To claim my shrinking hand as lawful wage
Of prowess in the battles of our house!

Could they not, kinder, send me to the grave
Rather than to that loathsome bridal bed?

Mother of God ! how did I let him live
To wake from nuptial sleep?

                I cannot breathe !
How close the night is !   Ah ! sweet rose, in rain
And darkness waiting all this lone night through,
Is love its own solution?   Does the heart
That wakes love prove itself worthy of love?
Thus prove itself from essence holy, high,
By destiny divine create for love?
You love your nightingale, and question not
For proof of worth ; and I, because I love,
Love on, and love and love !

                A little thing
It were in my lord's wine — no Venice glass
Is his — to mix a drop of death, which Time
Already pours, but with how slow a hand !
'T is not the doing !   You, my blood-red rose,
Would gladly cast those vivid petals, wet
With tears of waiting, 'twixt your winged one's breast
And threatening thorns ; but by that very deed

Would spoil the rose he loves.   If love be true,
To sacrifice all self for love, defeats
Love's best fruition.   On those endless years
Of burning pain that the monks prate, slow scorn
Well could I smile to give my prince a joy
One short, keen moment long !   But to abase
Myself from what I am, would be to spoil
The rose he worships.

                  Yet might I be free !
Might I but walk without the creeping dread
Of hearing on the path the slow, cool step
Of well-assured possession !   I have been
Upon the very brink of bitter death,
Because that step's assumption could not there
Come following me ; and but the poignant thought
That there another step would miss me too,
Has held me back.   Great God ! were I but free !
If on the morrow when his wine shall set
His lordship dozing, he sleep on and on,
My widow's tears would lack the angry salt
That galled the bride's cheek on my wedding-day !

Yet thus I were not free !   'T were but exchange
Of certainty for doubt.   Suppose my prince

Some fearful midnight — dark, perchance, as this —
Should start from dreaming that it was *his* wine
I tampered with !

             No more this vial holds
My hope, but my most deadly dread !   O sweet !
It is for love's sake that I here resign
The key to love's dominion.   As I break
This vase, it is not hope, but fear, I spill ;
For hope lives on because I love you still !

University Press : John Wilson & Son, Cambridge.